espresso
education

Phonics

Kim's Joke

Gill Budgell

W
FRANKLIN WATTS
LONDON•SYDNEY

First published in 2012 by
Franklin Watts
338 Euston Road
London NW1 3BH

Franklin Watts Australia
Level 17/207 Kent Street
Sydney NSW 2000

Text and illustration © Franklin Watts 2012

The Espresso characters are originated and
designed by Claire Underwood and Pesky Ltd.

The Espresso characters are the property of
Espresso Education Ltd.

A CIP catalogue record for this book is
available from the British Library.

ISBN: 978 1 4451 0747 9 (hbk)
ISBN: 978 1 4451 0750 9 (pbk)

Illustrations by Artful Doodlers Ltd.
Art Director: Jonathan Hair
Series Editor: Jackie Hamley
Project Manager: Gill Budgell
Series Designer: Matthew Lilly

Printed in China

Franklin Watts is a division of
Hachette Children's Books,
an Hachette UK company.

www.hachette.co.uk

Level 1 50 words
Concentrating on CVC words plus and, the, to

Level 2 70 words
Concentrating on double letter sounds and new letter
sounds (ck, ff, ll, ss, j, v, w, x, y, z, zz) plus no, go, I

Level 3 100 words
Concentrating on new graphemes (qu, ch, sh, th, ng,
ai, ee, igh, oa, oo, ar, or, ur, ow, oi, ear, air, ure, er)
plus he, she, we, me, be, was, my, you, they, her, all

Level 4 150 words
Concentrating on adjacent consonants (CVCC/CCVC
words) plus said, so, have, like, some, come, were, there,
little, one, do, when, out, what

Level 5 180 words
Concentrating on new graphemes (ay, wh, ue, ir, ou, aw,
ph, ew, ea, a-e, e-e, i-e, o-e, u-e) plus day, very, put, time,
about, saw, here, came, made, don't, asked, looked,
called, Mrs

Level 6 200 words
Concentrating on alternative pronunciations (c, ow, o, g, y)
and spellings (ee, ur, ay, or, m, n, air, l, r) plus your, don't
time, saw, here, very, make, their, called, asked, looked

Kim's hair was too long.
"You need a haircut,"
said Mum.

"But Ash has come to play today," said Kim.

They drove to
Mrs Luke's home.
"Come in," said Mrs
Luke. "Call me June."

"What can I do
for you boys? Blue hair,
red hair or just a trim?"
she joked.

June got a blue gown
for Kim to put on.
"Here's the spray to wet
your hair," she said.

"Now sit as still
as a statue.
That's the rule!"

"If I cut too much off
then we can use the glue
to stick it back on,"
joked June.

"And have a tissue in case I nip your ear!" June was very funny.

"Why don't we play a joke
on Kim's mum?" Ash asked.

He chose a white wig
for Kim to put on.
"I hope your mum
likes a joke," said June.

"Oh Kim! What a huge shock!" said Mum. But it was a fun way to end the day.

Puzzle Time

Match the words to the picture if they have the same sound in them. One has been done for you.

Look out! They might be different letters but sound the same.

win

tr<u>ay</u>

road

June

stat<u>ue</u>

sail

joke

white

b<u>o</u>n<u>e</u>

zoo

<u>w</u>hale

day

23

Answers

wait – gate is already completed to show the first pair.

chase and **mail** are also both **/ai/**
bee, tree, even, lead are all **/ee/**
hoop, flew, screw, spoon are all long **/oo/**

A note about the phonics in this book

Concentrating on new phonemes
In this book children practise reading new graphemes (letters) for some phonemes (sounds) that they already know. For example, they already know that the letters ee make the /ee/ sound but now they are practising that ea and e-e can also make the /ee/ sound.

Known phoneme	New graphemes	Words in the story
/ai/	a-e	came, chase, late, gate, take
/ee/	ea	stream, please, lead, leave, leap,
		clean
/ee/	e-e	these, even
/oo/	ew	threw, chew, flew
common words	here, came, don't	
tricky common words	called	

Remind children about the letters they already know for these phonemes.

In the puzzle they are challenged to match the words that have the same sound in them; the same sound but different letters.

Top tip: if a child gets stuck on a word then ask them to try and sound it out and then blend it together again or show them how to do this. For example, stream, s-t-r-ea-m, stream.